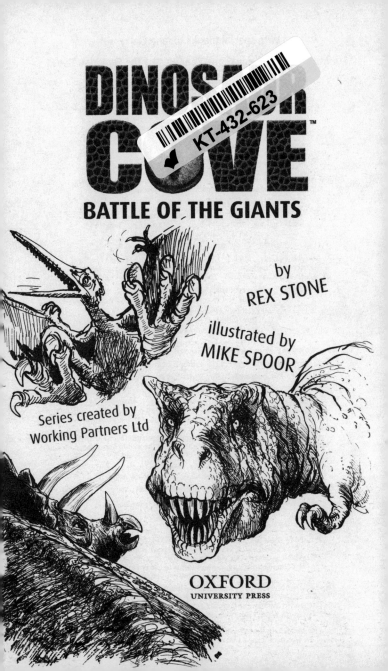

DINOSAUR COVE™

BATTLE OF THE GIANTS

by
REX STONE

illustrated by
MIKE SPOOR

Series created by
Working Partners Ltd

KT-432-623

OXFORD
UNIVERSITY PRESS

With special thanks to Jane Clarke

For Mackenzie, Benedict, and Charles, aka The Snowdon Boys

To a very special *Dinosaur Cove* fan
Tyler Dempsey-Ridley
Happy reading!

OXFORD
UNIVERSITY PRESS

Great Clarendon Street, Oxford OX2 6DP

Oxford University Press is a department of the University of Oxford.
It furthers the University's objective of excellence in research, scholarship,
and education by publishing worldwide in

Oxford   New York

Auckland   Cape Town   Dar es Salaam   Hong Kong   Karachi
Kuala Lumpur   Madrid   Melbourne   Mexico City   Nairobi
New Delhi   Shanghai   Taipei   Toronto

With offices in

Argentina   Austria   Brazil   Chile   Czech Republic   France   Greece
Guatemala   Hungary   Italy   Japan   Poland   Portugal   Singapore
South Korea   Switzerland   Thailand   Turkey   Ukraine   Vietnam

Oxford is a registered trade mark of Oxford University Press
in the UK and in certain other countries

British Library Cataloguing in Publication Data

Data available

ISBN: 978-0-9562877-2-4

1-3-5-7-9-10-8-6-4-2

Printed in Great Britain by Cox and Wyman Ltd, Reading, Berkshire
Paper used in the production of this book is a natural,
recyclable product made from wood grown in sustainable forests
The manufacturing process conforms to the environmental
regulations of the country of origin

This book has been specially written and published for World Book Day 2010.
World Book Day is a worldwide celebration of books and reading, with events
held last year in countries as far apart as Afghanistan and Australia, Nigeria and
Uruguay. For further information please see **www.worldbookday.com**
World Book Day in the UK and Ireland is made possible by generous sponsorship
from National Book Tokens, participating publishers, authors and booksellers.
Booksellers who accept the £1 World Book Day Token kindly agree to bear the full
cost of redeeming it

FACT FILE

TRICERATOPS

- **FULL NAME:** TRICERATOPS
- **AGE:** 65 – 80 MILLION YEARS**
- **SIZE:** 2 JATOMS*
- **LENGH:** 6 JATOMS*
- **WEIGHT:** 280 JATOMS*
- **LIKES:** BEING ONE OF THE HERD
- **DISLIKES:** BECOMING EXTINCT. IT WAS ONE OF THE LAST TO GO

Triceratops's foot

Triceratops's horns

T-REX

- **FULL NAME:** TYRANNOSAURUS REX
- **AGE:** 65 – 80 MILLION YEARS**
- **SIZE:** 5 JATOMS*
- **LENGTH:** 10 JATOMS*
- **WEIGHT:** 200 JATOMS*
- **LIKES:** FRESH FLESH AND CRUNCHING BONES
- **DISLIKES:** OTHER T-REX

T-Rex's teeth

T-Rex's eye

*NOTE: A JATON IS THE SIZE OF JAMIE OR TOM: 125 CM TALL AND 27 KG IN WEIGHT
**NOTE: SCIENTISTS CALL THIS PERIOD THE LATE CRETACEOUS

'Dinosaur Cove! The best place in the world to discover dinosaurs!' Jamie Morgan declared, throwing his arms open. He and his best friend, Tom Clay, were standing at Smuggler's Point, looking out over the bay.

'That's what it says on the new sign over the entrance to your dad's dinosaur museum!' Tom exclaimed, focusing his binoculars on the old lighthouse on the opposite headland. 'Are you sure your dad doesn't know about the *real* dinosaurs *we've* discovered?'

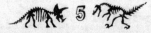

'Sure I'm sure, you wombat! It's top
secret!' Jamie grinned. Only he and Tom
knew that right here, in Dinosaur Cove, they
had found the entrance to a world of living,
breathing prehistoric creatures. Any minute
now, they'd be visiting that world again.

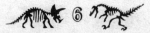

They scrambled down to the entrance to the smugglers' cave. Jamie rummaged in his backpack and flicked on his torch.

'Got the key?' Tom asked him.

'Check!' Jamie pulled out the late-Cretaceous ammonite that he'd found on the beach on his first day in Dinosaur Cove. He and Tom had worked out that the fossil they carried with them was the magic key to the prehistoric time period they visited. They'd had amazing adventures in the Jurassic and the Ice Age, and now they'd decided go back to the Cretaceous where they'd first encountered living, breathing, stomping, chomping dinosaurs.

The two friends raced down the cave and squeezed through the hidden gap at the

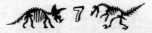 7

back into the smaller, darker, secret cave.
Jamie's heart thumped with excitement
as his torch picked out the rare fossilized
dinosaur footprints that led across the
damp stone floor.

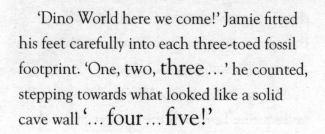

'Dino World here we come!' Jamie fitted
his feet carefully into each three-toed fossil
footprint. 'One, two, three…' he counted,
stepping towards what looked like a solid
cave wall '…four…five!'

There was a blinding
flash of light and Jamie's
foot squished into a fresh,
muddy dinosaur footprint.
Squelch!

Another second, and
Tom was beside him,
blinking in the warm
sunlight. Outside the
shallow cave was a bright
jungle of trees with fan-
shaped yellow-green
leaves, hung with dark
green vines. The hot,
humid air throbbed with
the buzzing of huge insects,
strange squawks, roars,
and distant trumpeting
bellows.

Jamie's heart leapt.
They were in Dino World
again!

The two friends stepped out of the cave—
onto a pile of orange mush that looked and
smelt like carrot sick.

'Phwoar!' Jamie said, gagging. 'The
gingkoes are ripe!'

He saw a green-brown creature, the size
of a large dog, burst out of the gingko trees.
It ran on its hind legs and hurled itself
at him.

'Ooof!' Jamie landed flat on his back in the
foul-smelling goo. The little dinosaur bobbed
its bony head up and down, and licked off the

slime that spattered Jamie. 'Gerroff!' Jamie
mumbled, struggling to his feet.

'Wanna!' Tom was laughing. 'You were
lying in wait for us!'

The little wannanosaurus cocked his head to one side. Then he bounded up to Tom on his hind legs, wagging his tail. Tom bent to pat him.

Sluuurp! Wanna's long, sandpapery tongue was loaded with stinky gingko drool.

'Gross!' Tom spluttered, wiping his freckly face on his sleeve.

Jamie plucked a ripe fruit from a gingko tree and gave it to the little dinosaur. Wanna grunked happily as he guzzled his favourite treat. Jamie and Tom grinned at each other. It was Wanna's fossilized footprints that brought them into Dino World, and their dinosaur friend came with them on all their adventures.

Wanna licked the last drop of stinky gingko juice from his scaly chin and bounded off into the trees.

'Wait for us, Wanna!' Jamie called.

The boys raced after the little dinosaur, pushing aside creepers until they burst out at the viewpoint at the edge of the cliff.

Below them lay late-Cretaceous Dino World. Jamie caught his breath, remembering the amazing adventures they'd had there.

'Awesome!' Tom breathed, focusing his binoculars on the Great Plains. 'I can see eddies! And a herd of T-tops!' He handed the binoculars to Jamie.

It's great to be back in the Cretaceous, Jamie thought. On the far side of the plains, he could make out a huge edmontosaurus stretching its neck to reach the tastiest

young branches of a conifer tree. Closer to them, seven triceratops lumbered towards the shelter of the jungle.

'It looks safe. No sign of any meat eaters,' he said, handing the binoculars back to Tom.

'Don't you want to see another T-Rex?' Tom teased him.

'Only if it doesn't see us first!' Jamie retorted. Then the three friends scrambled down the steep slope that led into the world of the dinosaurs.

CHAPTER 3

Jamie, Tom, and Wanna strode through
the steamy Cretaceous jungle, pushing aside
the dripping tree ferns and emerald green
vines that hung from mighty conifers.
Close to the river, the spongy ground
became soggier.

'It must be the wet season,' Jamie
commented, squishing through the muddy
ooze. He held his backpack above his head
and waded into the warm river.

'No kidding, fossil brain!' said Tom. Water
was swirling around the top of his legs.

Wanna leapt in with a splash.

'Thanks for the shower, Wanna!' Tom spluttered.

They sloshed across the swollen river. Ahead of them, three young ankylosaurs, the size of cars, were struggling to heave their huge armoured bodies up the slippery river bank. The biggest one thumped the bony club on the end of its tail into the mud with frustration. Sludge rained down over its companions.

Arooop! they complained.

'Mud's hard work when you're as heavy as an anky!' Jamie laughed, watching them heave themselves out and disappear into the jungle. Luckily, he, Tom, and Wanna were light enough to clamber easily onto firmer ground. The friends shook themselves dry like Wanna.

A well-trampled dinosaur trackway led from the river bank into the jungle. 'Lots of plant-eaters use this,' Tom declared, standing in a tyre-sized footprint.

'Any sign of big claw prints?' Jamie asked, looking round. 'From a you-know-who-saurus?'

'Is that the same as a do-you-think-he-saurus?' Tom asked.

'Let's just call it terror-chops!' Jamie joked nervously.

'You've got T-Rex on the brain!' Tom muttered, examining the ground. 'I can't see any meat-eater prints. Come on!'

They followed the trackway through the thick green jungle that rang with the squawks of pterodactyls and archaeopteryx.

As they rounded a jumble of rocks at the base of a steep hill, the ground beneath their feet began to rumble.

Wanna bobbed his head up and down in alarm.

'Get out of the way!' Tom yelled. 'Something's coming!'

Jamie and Tom scrambled onto a flat rock that overlooked the trackway.

Gruuunk! Wanna's feet scrabbled at the overhang. The boys leaned over and grabbed the little dinosaur by his scaly arms and hauled him up.

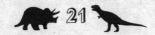

Grunk! Wanna murmured
nervously. *Grunk, grunk.*
He flattened himself
to the rock and peered
out over the edge. Tom
and Jamie did the same.

The rumbling noise was
joined by a low mooing.
Jamie recognized it instantly.
'T-tops!' he whispered.

A massive beaked head with three
horns appeared. An elephant-sized
triceratops stomped past. Jamie caught

his breath. It was so close he could reach out and touch the thick scaly frill that protected its neck.

Snurf!

Jamie jumped as a great snort came from the jungle trees behind them. A blast of slime splattered the back of his neck and the smell of rotting flesh welled up around him. Jamie rolled onto his back …

… and looked up through the leaves at the underside of enormous green scaly jaws, lined with dagger-like fangs. Jamie's stomach gave a somersault. Right above them was the dinosaur he feared the most. The lizard king. Tyrannosaurus Rex!

The T-Rex withdrew into the trees, but the vicious predator hadn't gone away; Jamie could still hear it breathing. Tom and Wanna were quivering with terror. Jamie knew he was shaking too.

'Don't make any sudden moves,' Tom hissed. 'It hasn't seen us!'

'What's it doing?' Jamie struggled to lie still as a foul-smelling glob of dino drool plopped into his ear.

'It's lying in wait for T-tops,' Tom whispered. 'It's an ambush!'

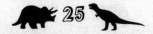

Jamie's heart was in his mouth as he listened to the triceratops plod along the trackway.

Aaaark! A screech came from overhead. A quetzalcoatlus the size of a small aeroplane swooped towards them, claws out like a fishing eagle. Jamie froze. It was going to carry him off! But the huge pterosaur screeched again and soared away on its leathery wings.

'It must have sensed the Rex,' Tom murmured.

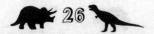

Slowly, Jamie rolled onto his stomach and looked down. Seven triceratops were lumbering off along the trackway. The last had just passed under the rocky ledge. They were nearly out of danger.

'The last one's stopped!' Tom groaned.

Jamie stared as the huge triceratops stuck its beaky nose into a patch of juicy purple leaves. It was bigger than a bull elephant, with three powerful horns and a frill the size of a dinner table. Jamie willed it to move away safely, but it stood chomping. He could hear its fat stomach gurgling. Suddenly, the jungle went quiet. Beside him, Wanna shivered. The T-tops paused mid-chew.

Raar!

With an almighty roar, the T-Rex leapt over them. It was as long as a bus! The enormous tiger-striped predator launched itself at the T-tops, sinking its fangs into the other dinosaur's leg and scrabbling to grip the plant-eater's bony frill with its vicious claws.

27

The T-tops bellowed and reared up. It side-slammed the Rex, then tried to run away. But the Rex blocked its path and unhinged its powerful jaws.'

'Let's get out of here!' Jamie hissed, but Tom was transfixed.

'It dislocated its jaws like a snake,' Tom whispered. 'T-tops is history.'

Raaar!

The T-Rex sprang at the T-tops, but the T-tops tossed its head just managing to block the predator with its bony frill. Blood dripped from a bite wound on the triceratops's frill.

'I can't watch,' Jamie groaned.

'It's the law of the jungle,' Tom whispered. 'Meat-eaters have to eat.'

The T-Rex and the T-tops stood eye to eye. Suddenly the T-Rex span round. Its tail caught the T-tops under its chin and sent it sprawling across the trackway. The T-tops lay on its side, revealing its soft underbelly.

'Oh no!' Jamie jumped to his feet as the T-Rex unhinged its fearsome jaws again to deliver the killer bite.

'That's not fighting fair, you big bully!' Jamie yelled.

'Shush, fossil brain,' Tom hissed. 'It'll hear you.'

Too late.

The T-Rex looked up.

CHAPTER 5

SEARCH

The T-tops scrambled to its feet.

Whump! It side-slammed the T-Rex, knocking it over so that it crumpled to the ground with an earth shaking

Thud!

'Go T-tops!' Jamie and Tom cheered as the triceratops charged back down the path. The T-Rex glanced towards them. They flattened themselves to the rock as it struggled to its feet, roaring and snarling with rage. The Rex sped, limping, after its prey.

'Do you think
T-tops will get away?'
Jamie asked.

'There's only one
way to find out,' Tom
said. 'Follow them!'
He scrambled down
the rocks and raced
after the retreating
T-tops. Jamie dashed
after him. He glanced
over his shoulder.
Wanna was trailing
reluctantly behind.

Ahead of them, the
T-tops zigzagged back
down the trackway,
crashing in and out of
the trees to dodge the
T-Rex's snapping jaws.
As soon as it came to a
clearing in the jungle

trees, it whirled around to face its hunter. The two huge dinosaurs circled each other, trampling a ring into the damp leaf-mould.

The boys and Wanna peered out from behind a fallen tree trunk that sprouted weird purple fungus.

'T-tops is as good as dino-dinner!' Tom exclaimed.

'T-tops isn't as tall as the Rex, but it's more solid,' Jamie retorted. 'It has a good chance.'

'It's a T-Rex versus T-tops battle of the giants,' Tom said in his wildlife TV commentator voice, 'and we're in the ringside seats.' He began to speak quickly to keep up with the action.

'T-tops is trying to use those sharp horns to gore the Rex, but the Rex snaps with its ferocious jaws ... Phew! That was close. T-tops dodges, lowering its head. It's charging the Rex! The Rex looks as if it can't believe it! It sidesteps ... Ow! That horn in the side must have hurt. T-tops follows it up with a side slam. And he's down! T-Rex is down! Round Two goes to T-tops!'

Jamie watched the T-Rex struggle to its feet as the T-tops trudged away.

'It's not over yet,' he told Tom.

 Snarling, the tyrannosaurus limped towards the triceratops. 'They're getting

tired,' Tom said. 'The Rex is having to work hard for its dinner.'

Grunk! Wanna tugged at Jamie's backpack.

'We can't go yet. I want to see T-tops get away,' Jamie told him.

Wanna's grunks became more insistent.

Grunk, grunk, grunk!

The T-Rex turned its head slowly towards them and sniffed deeply. The red crests over its yellow eyes flashed.

'Uh-uh!' Tom gasped. 'It's sniffed out something easier to eat. Us!'

'Run for it!' Tom yelled.

The boys and Wanna sprinted off with
T-Rex limping after. They zigzagged in and
out of the trees like the triceratops, but it
was no good. When Jamie dared to look over
his shoulder, he could see that T-Rex was
gaining on them.

'Head for the river,' Jamie panted. 'The
Rex is so heavy, it will get bogged down!'

They scrambled down the river bank
and waded across. Behind them, the T-Rex
plunged into the water. It was so close, they

could feel its stinking
breath on the
back of their
necks. They threw
themselves onto
the mud on the
other side of
the river.

Squelch. The
T-Rex's heavy feet sank in the ooze as it
tried to get out. Jamie turned to see the
dinosaur dart its head towards them, but its
feet couldn't keep up.

'The mud's slowing it down!' he gasped.

The hungry T-Rex slogged after them, but
they could move quicker.

Raaar! it roared, as it watched them
get away.

Wanna turned back to the fearsome
creature and grunked crossly at it. The T-Rex
hung its head, exhausted.

'That told it!' Tom chuckled.

'We were nearly T-Rex's dinner!' Jamie panted. 'Just imagine if a scientist found some fossilized T-Rex dung and there were human bones in it!'

Tom and Jamie fell around laughing.

'Time to get back to Dinosaur Cove,' Jamie said at last. 'I'm as hungry as a T-Rex.'

They clambered back up the slope to Gingko Hill. At the top, they picked some ripe, stinky gingkoes for their dinosaur friend. Wanna stuffed them in his cheeks and settled down in his nest outside Gingko Cave with a contented sigh.

'See you on our next adventure, Wanna!' they told him, as they patted him goodbye.

Then they fitted their feet into Wanna's footprints and stepped backwards, feeling the prints turn to stone as they re-entered the dark secret cave. They squeezed through the gap into Smugglers' Cave, and came out into the bright salty air of Dinosaur Cove.

'That was an awesome battle!' Jamie grinned. 'I was right about T-tops. It got away.'

'But we nearly didn't,' Tom reminded him. 'I never want to get that close to T-Rex again!'

'Unless it's in my dad's museum!' Jamie laughed.

DINOSAUR WORLD

---- BOYS' ROUTE

Misty Lagoon

White Ocean

44

Far Away Mountains

Crashing
Rock
Falls

Great Plains

Fang
Rock

Jungle

Gingko
Hill

45

WHY NOT READ SOME MORE DINOSAUR COVE ADVENTURES...

JURASSIC

7 — DINOSAUR COVE — Rescuing the Plated Lizard — Rex Stone

8 — DINOSAUR COVE — Swimming with the Sea Monster — Rex Stone

9 — DINOSAUR COVE — Tracking the Gigantic Beast — Rex Stone

10 — DINOSAUR COVE — Escape from the Fierce Predator — Rex Stone

11 — DINOSAUR COVE — Finding the Deceptive Dinosaur — Rex Stone

12 — DINOSAUR COVE — Assault of the Friendly Fiends — Rex Stone

TRIASSIC

13 — DINOSAUR COVE — Chasing the Tunnelling Trickster — Rex Stone

14 — DINOSAUR COVE — Clash of the Monster Crocs — Rex Stone

15 — DINOSAUR COVE — Rampage of the Hungry Giants — COMING SOON

16 — DINOSAUR COVE — Haunting of the Ghost Runners — Rex Stone — COMING SOON

If you're Dotty about

DINOSAURS

and round the bend about

REPTILES,

you'll love the

DINOSAUR COVE™

website

www.dinosaurcove.co.uk

**FLIP OVER
FOR ANOTHER
GREAT READ**

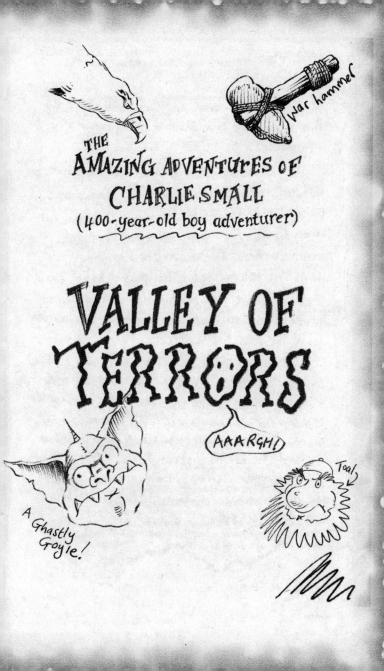

If you find this book, PLEASE look after it. This is the only true account of my remarkable adventures.

My name is Charlie Small and I am four hundred years old, but in all those long years I have never grown up. Something happened when I was eight years old, something I can't begin to understand. I went on a journey... and I'm still trying to find my way home. Now, although I have had four hundred years of perilous adventures, I still look like any eight-year-old boy you might pass in the street.

I've travelled to the ends of the earth and to the centre of the earth. I've been kidnapped; crowned king of gorillas; fought fearsome monsters and ~~plundered~~ plundered a mummy's tomb! You may think this sounds fantastic; you could think it's a lie. But you would be wrong, because EVERYTHING IN MY JOURNALS IS TRUE. Believe this single fact and you can share the most incredible journey ever experienced. Charlie Small

BURP!

A belching burble

PUBLISHER'S NOTE:

These torn and smudged pages are from one of Charlie Small's fantastic journals. A school dinner lady found them in the greasy gunk behind an old oven. How on earth did they end up there? If you find any more loose pages, *please let us know!*

NAME: Charlie Small

ADDRESS: Highlands of Horroscar

AGE: 400 (I'm older than my granny)

MOBILE: 077131238

SCHOOL: St. Beckham's

THINGS I LIKE: Smuts; The Buzz-Saw Buzzard; The Horroscar clan

THINGS I HATE: Giant goats; Goyles!

THE AMAZING ADVENTURES OF CHARLIE SMALL: VALLEY OF TERRORS
A DAVID FICKLING BOOK
978 0 956 28772 4

Published in Great Britain by David Fickling Books
a division of Random House Children's Books
A Random House Group Company

This edition published specially for World Book Day 2010

1 3 5 7 9 10 8 6 4 2

Set in 14/16 Garamond MT

DAVID FICKLING BOOKS
31 Beaumont Street, Oxford, OX1 2NP

www.**davidficklingbooks**.co.uk
www.**rbooks**.co.uk

Addresses for companies within The Random House Group Limited can be found at:
www.randomhouse.co.uk/offices.htm

THE RANDOM HOUSE GROUP Limited Reg. No. 954009
A CIP catalogue record for this book is available from the British Library.

Printed and bound in Great Britain by Cox and Wyman Ltd, Reading, Berkshire

This book has been specially written and published for World Book Day 2010.
World Book Day is a worldwide celebration of books and reading,
with events held last year in countries part as far apart as
Afghanistan and Australia, Nigeria and Uruguay.
For further information please see **www.worldbookday.com**
World Book Day in the UK and Ireland is made possible by generous sponsorship
from National Book Tokens, participating publishers, authors and booksellers.
Booksellers who accept the £1 World Book Day Token
kindly agree to bear the full cost of redeeming it.

Walking A Dangerous Path

Such a lot has happened since I escaped the clutches of a bunch of belching Burbles. These annoying, dribbling creatures tracked me over moors, chased me across dusty wastelands, and shadowed my every move until I finally lost them in the rugged foothills of a place known as the Highlands of Horroscar.

Ahead, the land climbed to form rows of great rocky hills and brooding mountains. The wind whistled, and a screeching eagle patrolled the lonely sky as I took a narrow path that weaved its way up the side of a towering, flat-topped peak. My feet were sore and my tummy rumbled with hunger.

Directly below me was a deep valley like a jagged crack in the earth's crust. The bottom was hidden below layers of swirling mist and I shuddered – what a place! One wrong step on this precarious path and I would discover just how deep the valley was.

The path turned a sharp corner and I stepped forward and . . . Whoa! A loop of string tightened around my ankle and a jerk

A loop of string! (watch out!)

sent me tumbling over.
I tried to scramble to
my feet, but something
heavy leaped on my back
and pushed me down.

'Geroff!' I croaked, through a mouthful
of dust.

'Blimey, you're a boy!' said a gravelly voice
and I was immediately released. I jumped to
my feet and turned to face my attacker. A
grubby face grinned at me.

'*You're* a boy!' I said in surprise.

'Tha's right,' the boy said, his voice as
rough as sandpaper. He was
about my age and wore a
leather kilt down to his knees,
with a rough hairy waistcoat
over his bare chest. His
feet were filthy and
his face, half hidden
under a thick
thatch of dark
hair, was
not much
cleaner.

'Quick, in here!' he said and jostled me

towards a shallow cave in the mountain wall.

'What's going on?' I asked.

'It's not safe. Get inside,' the muddy boy replied, pushing me forwards.

Attack From The Sky

As we stepped into the gloom, the boy said, "S all right, Quinn. 'S only a bitty boy.' At the rear of the cave I saw a two-year-old boy sitting on a pile of loose stones. He was a stocky little chap with a wide, flat-featured face and dressed in leather dungarees. This is a strange place to bring a defenceless baby, I thought. But to my amazement, the toddler gurgled, picked up a rock the size of a football and lifted it above his head.

'Biff!' he cried, and heaved it across the cave as easily as if it were made of cardboard. He grinned and lifted his arms in triumph. 'Biffety bop!'

'That's incredible!' I exclaimed. 'That rock must weigh a ton!'

'We don't call him the Mighty Quinn for nothing!' smiled the shock-haired boy. Then he added, 'Look, I'm sorry about attacking you. We thought you was a goyle!'

'A girl? I don't look anything like a girl,' I exclaimed. 'You're the one wearing a skirt!' (I know my hair has grown pretty long over the last four hundred years, but really!)

'Not a girl,' said the boy with a grin. 'A goyle! My name's Smuts, by the way.'

'I'm Charlie. Charlie Small. What on earth's a goyle?' I asked, but before the boy could reply, a terrific noise filled the small cave.

'Hide, Quinn. The demon's found us!' Smuts yelled, as a scary flapping creature landed in the mouth of the cave. The bird-like thing was hardly any bigger than Quinn, with mottled blue skin and a floppy, purplish tongue that made it look rather stupid. It had long arms, two large wings and was squatting on a pair of hairy, cloven-footed legs. A cracked horn grew from the centre of its forehead.

With staring eyes, it slowly began to creep forward towards Quinn. Smuts stepped into

the creature's path, but with one shove of its horned head, the pint-sized pest sent him sprawling in the dirt.

'Don't let it pass!' he gasped, winded.

'Get back, you ugly brute!' I growled, flapping my arms at the fiend and trying to sound menacing. The thing cocked its head on one side and looked at me with a pair of pale, goggle-eyes. Yikes, what a creature!

Then it took a deep breath, opened its jaws and . . . I waited for an ear-splitting, earth-shaking lion's roar, but, *'Honk!'* the creature rasped like a silly goose. The noise was so comical that I burst out laughing.

~HONK!

Suddenly a powerful jet of rusty water spouted from its mouth and hit me on the chest. *Oof!* I rocketed back and landed with a bump on my backside.

'Ouch!' I yelled, rubbing my bruised bum.

Then the mini monster grabbed Quinn, tucked him under one arm, and raced from the cave.

Hanging By My Fingertips (Aaargh!)

'Stop it!' yelled Smuts, hurrying to his feet and tearing after the pilfering pest. I followed hot on his heels, but as we emerged on to the path, the beast flapped its wide wings, honked like a clown's car and leaped from the ledge.

'Fun!' the toddler cried as they rose into the air. 'Biffety bop!'

The older boy dived, catching hold of one of the creature's ankles. 'Come back, you goon!' he yelled.

'*Honk!*' beeped the predator thrashing its wings frantically but unable to rise any higher. It spurted out another jet of water.

'Hold on!' I yelled and ran over to help bring the beast down. As I did so, the edge of the path gave way beneath my feet and with a cry I fell over the brink towards the deep valley below. My fingers scrabbled at the crumbling rock until they found a narrow ledge, and there I hung, dangling over a sheer and dizzying drop. My fingers began to slip.

'Help!' I yelled as my grip gave way entirely . . . but just as I dropped, a strong hand clamped itself around my wrist. I looked up and saw Smut's face looking back at me. With a mighty heave he hauled me back onto the path.

Above us, a dark shape carrying a

Fun!

wriggling bundle climbed silently into the sky before turning and gliding down into the misty valley. We could hear Quinn's voice fading away, chortling 'Bye bye! Bye bye!' over and over.

'Wow, thanks!' I panted, sitting down and taking a deep breath. 'But you let that thing escape with Quinn in order to save me!'

'I couldn't hold it any longer,' said the boy, mournfully.

'What the heck was it?' I asked.

''Twas a goyle! It's been tracking us most of the mornin'. That's why I attacked you – I thought *you* was the goyle,' said Smuts, breathless. He looked out at the disappearing beast. 'It's too late to go after him now – it'll be dark soon. I'm not worried about Quinn; he's not scared of anything and the goyles won't harm him. It's Quinn's dad they really want – Toal Horroscar, our mighty leader. They know he'll try and rescue the lad.' Smuts looked terrified now. 'Oh, cripes! I've got to tell Toal what's happened – and he's got a temper like a roaring volcano!'

'It's not *your* fault,' I said. 'You tried your best to stop the goyle.'

'Yeah, but I'm supposed to be Quinn's sort of . . . nanny!' Smuts explained, looking embarrassed. 'But the little so-and-so gave me the slip, *again*! He's always running off and getting into scrapes – this morning I found him halfway down the mountain, goyle-spotting. Oh, darn it! Look, Charlie, I know it's a lot to ask, but would you come with me and back up my story – explain to Toal it wasn't my fault?'

'Oh, er . . . OK,' I said. I didn't relish the thought of meeting a human volcano called Horroscar, but I did feel a bit responsible for Quinn being taken. If I hadn't slipped and if Smuts hadn't come to my rescue, we might have been able to save the little boy.

The Legend Of The Goyles

We set off along the steep path that carried on up the mountainside. Eventually we came to a rocky plateau where a narrow waterfall cascaded down from the cliff face above, splashing over rocks where tiny pink flowers blossomed. Crossing the slippery rocks at the base, I followed Smuts as he climbed up the side of the waterfall, looking nervously at the sky for signs of circling goyles.

'What exactly are goyles?' I asked. 'That creature looked just like the carvings on old church roofs.'

'That's what they are – gargoyles, but we call 'em goyles for short.'

'But gargoyles are made of stone,' I said.

'And so they are,' said Smuts. 'Many centuries ago, a dark magician came this way, searching for a special stone to build his magical mansion with. Deep in the valley below, he found a rare blue rock and used it to carve into gross gargoyles for his roof. Then one day there was a terrible storm. Bolts of lightning shot from rolling black clouds and tore down into the valley. The mysterious magician was never seen again, but every goyle came instantly to life.'

'Blimey!' I said. 'Is that true?'

'That's the legend,' said Smuts, stretching for a handhold. 'The stone creatures have terrorized the highlands ever since. That's why it's called the Valley of Terrors and it's why we now live so high up. It's harder for the goyles to breathe up here.'

'Jeepers!' I said, puffing to try and keep up with him. I could see why the goyles had trouble; the air was getting very thin and I was finding it hard to breathe too. 'This is a mighty long way for a toddler like Quinn to walk.'

'Oh, 'tis nothin' for the mighty Quinn,' said Smuts as he clambered on ahead. 'He's as strong and agile as a mountain goat.'

And Smuts was even stronger, as I was just about to witness, for as we clambered onto a broad ledge, the biggest goat I have ever seen appeared from behind a boulder. With a dreadful snort, the animal lowered his head and charged. YIKES!

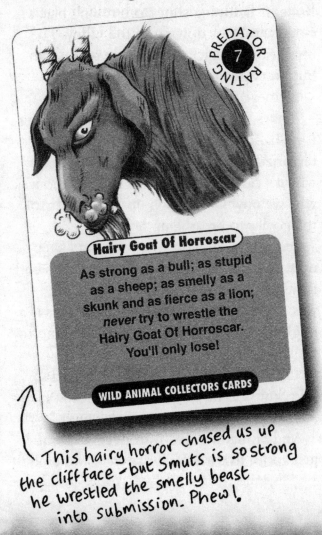

PREDATOR RATING 7

Hairy Goat Of Horroscar

As strong as a bull; as stupid as a sheep; as smelly as a skunk and as fierce as a lion; *never* try to wrestle the Hairy Goat Of Horroscar. You'll only lose!

WILD ANIMAL COLLECTORS CARDS

This hairy horror chased us up the cliff face - but Smuts is so strong he wrestled the smelly beast into submission. Phew!

Toal Horroscar

The sun was already beginning to set when we reached the flat crown of the topmost peak and arrived at Smut's home. It was a large village surrounded by a high wall of rocks. Above the wall I could see potbelly chimneys sending plumes of smoke into the clear air.

Smuts led the way towards a giant gate in the wall. Two tall look-out towers flanked the entrance and as we approached, a decrepit old guard blew a weak, wavering note on a strange-looking trumpet. The large doors slowly creaked open.

'Come on, Charlie, let's get it over with,' sighed Smuts as we entered a wide street that led us past rows of small shops. Groups of villagers were bartering for pots and grain, knobbly vegetables and hairy hides.

The clan's people had heavy jawlines, large crooked noses and stared menacingly at me from below thick bushy eyebrows. They wore simple smocks of leather or animal fur tied around the middle with rope, and their bare arms were knotted with muscle.

'Blimey, those men look ferocious!' I whispered.

'Those are Horroscar ladies, thank you very much!' said Smuts, offended.

Whoops, I thought. If that's what the women look like, how scary must the men be? But they all smiled and said friendly hellos to Smuts as we passed.

'So where are the men?' I asked.

'All been goyled,' said Smuts, stopping beside a very long barn at the end of the street. ''Cept for me 'n' Toal.'

'Bloomin' heck!' I said as Smuts rapped on the heavy wooden door.

'Ssshh!' he warned as the door opened and a huge man filled the entrance. He stood well over two metres high with a chest as broad as a tabletop. His brooding face was fringed by a shock of wild hair and a jutting, spade-shaped beard the colour of a rusty can. He was the biggest, most fearsome man I'd ever seen.

'Where's little Quinn – don't tell me you've lost him again?' he asked in a deep rumbling voice.

'I . . . er,'
hesitated Smuts.
'This is Charlie
Small . . .'

'Spit it out,
boy,' growled the
menacing chieftain.

Toal Horroscar
Yikes!

'Quinn's been
taken by the goyles,' said Smuts quickly.

Toal Horroscar's face flushed so dark
with anger I thought steam would come
shooting from his ears. *Taken?* he bellowed.
'You empty-headed eejit!' In one
swift movement he grabbed
Smuts and lifted him above his
head. Then, with a mighty heave
he launched the hapless boy into the air,
sending him helter-skeltering across the road
to land with a bump in the dust.

'Hold on,' I cried. 'It wasn't *his* fault.'

'Oh no? So whose fault was it then –
yours?' raged the giant, and lunged at me.
I managed to twist out of the way and ran
back a few paces.

'No way!' I said as the man-mountain
circled me, ready to make another strike.

19

'Quinn ran away to the Valley of Terrors! Smuts tracked him down but they were attacked on the way back. He tried his best to fight off the goyle. I know – I saw him!'

The gargantuan man stood staring at me in disbelief, shaking and rumbling ominously. I took another step back. Then, with a loud snort he tilted back his head and roared at the sky.

'Ha ha ha!' he bellowed. 'The little devil, running off by himself to fight the goyles! What a hero – just like his old man!' He shook with laughter. Then looking up at the darkening sky he added, 'Ah well, we'll have to rescue him tomorrow, Smuts. It's too late to go now.'

Blimey, I thought, that was a turnaround! 'Haven't you got anyone else to help you?' I asked, relieved.

'No one,' said Smuts, getting to his feet and hobbling over. 'The goyles have picked off all our soldiers one by one. Toal and I are the only warriors left in the village.'

'So, it's just us three, then?' I said rashly.

'Us *three*?' Smuts exclaimed. 'You mean you'll help us?'

'Well . . .' I said, already regretting my decision. Had I forgotten just how wicked that goyle was? Imagine what a flock of them would be like!

'Ha! You're a good man, Charlie Small,' bellowed Toal Horroscar before I could change my mind, and he gave me a friendly slap on the back that sent me sprawling in the dirt. 'And a brave one too, considering how deadly dangerous it's goin' to be! We'd better ask for guidance from the Great Sky God.' Then he added, 'First, though, I'd better tell the missus what's happened.'

He disappeared inside the house, and after a short silence an angry scream rent the air, followed by the sound of pots and pans crashing about. Toal appeared at the door looking shaken and flummoxed. Behind him a tiny, mouse-like woman stormed after him with a ladle in her hand.

'Calm down, Megan,'

Mrs Horroscar

pleaded her husband. 'I promise we'll go first thing in the morning.'

Megan stared at him frostily. 'If anything happens to me darlin' Quinn, I'll make mincemeat of you, you great hairy lummox. Fancy lettin' Smuts watch him after the *last* time!' she said, and slammed the door in Toal's face.

'Don't worry, my little horror,' Toal called after her. Then he muttered, 'Quick lads, follow me.'

The Great Sky God

The clan leader led us down a path behind the long barn to a dead-end at the village's defensive wall. Toal began pushing against one of the huge stones and a hidden door sprang open, revealing a flight of steps. We followed Toal down the steps. His huge shoulders scuffed both sides of the dark passage.

'What *is* this great sky god he's taking us to?' I whispered to Smuts.

'I've no idea,' the boy replied. 'He's never let anyone down here before. But he always asks the Sky God for advice when the clan is in trouble.'

Before long the corridor opened into a large cavern and I gasped at a breath-taking sight. The floor of the cave sloped steeply down to where the whole of one wall was open to the sky. The magnificent highland landscape was spread out below, the orange sun just dipping below a line of blue hills.

Against the opposite wall was the Sky God; a huge silver eagle of glittering steel that stood five metres high, with a great curved golden beak. It glowed in the shadows of the back wall.

Toal fell to his knees. 'Tell us what to do, oh Great God of the Sky,' he bellowed. 'Kneel!' he muttered testily to us. 'Show some respect.'

'That thing doesn't really speak, does it?' I whispered to Smuts. He shrugged his shoulders. Just then a gusting breeze swept into the cavern; chords of musical notes rose and fell with the wind, sounding just like a murmur of voices.

'Sshh!' whispered Toal, spreading out his arms. 'Can you hear it? It's sending us a message.'

This is ridiculous, I thought. It's only the wind making the metal feathers of the

I put myself in the picture to show just how big the sky god is!

bird vibrate; it's not actually *saying* anything. Then, as I studied the massive eagle more closely, I started to feel excited. The thing began to look vaguely familiar.

I got to my feet and trotted up to the giant eagle.

'Get back,' ordered Toal, looking terrified. 'You mustn't annoy the Sky God!'

'I won't be a mo,' I said and disappeared behind the idol.

'Charlie!' roared the chieftain. 'Get back here now!'

I ignored the fuming warrior as I studied the bird. Yep, there was no doubt about it now. It wasn't a statue of a sky god at all – it was one of my friend Jakeman's marvellous mechanimals!

Set into the eagle's back was a row of three open cockpits, the front one displaying a few simple dials and controls, and on a small riveted plate above its metal tail feathers were the faded words: Jakeman's Rubber-Band-Powered Buzz-Saw Buzzard. Hidden between the metal feathers were an instruction booklet and this piece of paper:

I've stuck it on the next page →

Jakeman's Rubber-Band-Powered
Buzz-Saw Buzzard

Wings in
take-off position

Pilot's cockpit

Windscreen

Powerful
crushing
beak

Steel head

Steel ball
amunition

Wing gun

Rubber-band

Take-off wheels

Go up, up and away in this

I flicked through the manual and smiled.
Oh boy, this was just the thing we needed.
Good old Jakeman!

I rushed out from behind the metal bird.

APPROVED JAKEMAN MECHANIMAL

Jakeman

IF IT DOESN'T HAVE MY SIGNATURE
IT WASN'T MADE BY ME

ACCEPT NO INFERIOR SUBSTITUTES

Passenger/fighter
Cockpits

Ejector Seats (in all cockpits)

Hammered steel body

Rubber-band-powered propeller
(Turn clockwise
2,324 times
to prime)

Smokescreen funnel

Buzz-saw

Buzz-saw hatch

beautiful machine!   Patent No. 60A

'You were right, Mr Horroscar,' I cried,
waving the machine's manual. 'Your sky god
has given us a message – look!'

'You dare to disobey Toal Horroscar?'

he yelled, 'I've a good mind to . . .' But just then the sound of a gong drifted into the cave. 'Ooh! That's Megan calling us for supper. Hurry up, we mustn't be late!' the great leader said, and hurried off down the passage like a huge naughty schoolboy.

The Night Before The Storm

The walls in the long barn were hung with staring goat heads, antelope horns and ugly war hammers. There were enough beds down either side for the *whole* village, and a huge oak table ran along the centre. The Horroscar ladies were laying the table and cutting hunks of bread. Smoke and steam billowed up to the rafters as Megan stirred a pot over a smelly peat fire that bathed the far end of the barn with a cosy glow.

'You're late,' she snapped as we rushed in.

'Sorry, my little horror,' the chief replied meekly. 'What delights have you cooked for us today?'

'Mountain lion stew,' she said, pouring a lumpy gloop into his bowl, complete with fangs, claws and eyeballs! 'Eat up. You'll need all your strength tomorrow to rescue my biddy baby.'

'Yes, my horror,' Toal mumbled.

'Here you are, Charlie, you poor skinny thing. You need some fat on yer bones,' said Megan and I slurped up a spoonful of the chewy stew. Mmm, would you believe it – mountain lion is delicious!

Toal continued to glower at me over his stew. As he gobbled down his food, I tried to tell him exactly what the metal bird was capable of. He didn't believe a word.

'What nonsense!' he scoffed, after I had finished explaining.

'It's true,' I said. 'Look!' and I showed him the manuals I keep in my rucksack of all the other Jakeman inventions that have helped me on my adventures.

'Are you sure it will work?' he grumbled.

'It's got to be worth a go, hasn't it?' said Smuts, excited.

'All right,' Toal grudgingly agreed. 'But if it all goes wrong, it's your fault, Charlie Small!'

Now I'm snug beneath a great fur blanket in the same long barn, surrounded by snoring highlanders and windy cattle – yes, the cows sleep here too and it's hard to work out who's the smellier – the animals or the Horroscar ladies!

I'm just finishing my journal by candlelight, before going to sleep. I've studied the manual from cover to cover and hope I've taken it all in, for tomorrow I have to pilot the great bird to the bottom of the Valley of Terrors. Wish me luck! I'll write more just as soon as I can.

Take-Off!

Oh boy, what a *petrifying* day! Let me explain what happened.

As the sun began to rise, Toal, Smuts and I collected some spears and war hammers.

'Now you be careful, ya big buffoon,' Megan said to her husband. 'I worry more about you than about our Quinn!'

'Yes, my little horror,' sighed Toal and gave her a tender parting kiss.

Once at the sky-cave, we used the lasso from my explorer's kit to lower the heavy bird onto its stomach. Reaching inside the front cockpit I yanked a lever. Four small wheels extended from the undercarriage, lifting the machine from the ground.

Next I turned the Buzzard's small propeller two thousand three hundred and twenty-four times to fully wind the thick rubber band that powered the flying machine.

'I hope you know what you're doing, Charlie,' said Smuts with wide, frightened eyes.

'Of course I do!' I fibbed.

'You'd better,' grumbled Toal gripping his massive war hammer as he climbed nervously into the rear cockpit. 'Or it's not the goyles that will have to watch out.'

I gulped and said, 'Just leave it to me. Nothing can go wrong.' I crossed my

fingers as I climbed into the pilot's seat and
prayed that the elastic band hadn't perished
or snapped. We put on our flying goggles
and clipped on our seatbelts. I checked my
rearview mirror and released the handbrake.

'Chocks away!' I cried as the heavy metal
hawk began to roll forward and rumble
down the slope towards the opening. Faster
and faster it trundled, bumping and bucking
over the uneven floor. Then, *whoosh!* we
careered out of the cave mouth.

'Yikes!'
I cried, my
stomach
flipping over.
'Help!' yelled
Smuts.
'Mummy!'
whimpered Toal.

Why aren't we flying? I wondered. Frantically I skimmed through the instruction booklet as the Buzzard dropped from the sky towards the craggy rocks below. So much for all my revision last night – my mind had gone completely blank!

'Aha! This should do it,' I shouted above the rushing wind, and pulled two handles on either side of my seat. The eagle's wings opened wide on a system of wires and pulleys and the mighty bird began to glide out of its dive. I pressed a button; the rear propeller spluttered into life and the machine slowly climbed upwards. Immediately a pre-recorded message from Jakeman crackled from a tinny speaker. *'Welcome to the flight of the eagle,'* his voice announced. *'We'll be cruising at approximately fifteen thousand feet. I hope you enjoy your trip.'*

'See, there's nothing to worry about,' I called.

Smuts and Toal didn't say anything. Their faces were frozen with terror!

Into The Valley Of Terrors

I steered the Buzzard down the shadowy valley, gliding from one end to the other, then turned and dropped for another sweep of the dark gorge. We descended through layers of cloud and clammy mist.

Then, all of a sudden, I saw six grisly gargoyles perched atop a series of jagged crags on either side of the narrow valley. As one, they took off and began to fly towards us.

Oooh!

They were like little grinning monkeys.

They looked like ugly little imps, about the size of small monkeys and full of malevolent mischief. One had wide flapping ears; another sported a long scaly tail and had a wide grin filled with sharp triangular teeth.

'Come on, ya gothic goons! Let's see what you're made of,' bellowed the great chieftain, undoing his seatbelt, standing up in the seat and swinging his mighty war hammer. The Buzzard rocked like a boat in a storm. Three of the goyles attacked from above, spraying tiny granite needles that flew from their mouths like swarms of angry wasps.

'Yeow!' Toal cried, crouching down in his cockpit for cover. Then: 'Come back and get what's coming to ya,' he roared as the goyles whooped and banked away. With a crash the other three goyles hit us from below like mini missiles, spinning the Buzzard and sending it into freefall. Yikes! I fought with the juddering steering column, desperately trying to regain control.

'Save us, oh Sky God!' cried Toal, clinging on for dear life.

Then, as I righted our rolling craft, one

of our wings slapped a goyle right on the bonce.

'*Gzzzz!*' it groaned, and like a stunned fly, span down to the valley floor. Shrieking excitedly the rest peeled away, overtaking us at incredible speed, and turned to attack from the front.

Good, I thought, this is where the mechanical Buzzard comes into its own!

A Nest Of Goyles

The five goyles raced straight towards us.

I quickly flicked a switch to expose two short gun muzzles in the Buzzard's wings and pressed the FIRE button on the steering wheel. The guns rattled into life, spitting out shiny

BANG!

sticky string!

silver balls that exploded in the air like party poppers, coating two of the goyles with sticky strings that instantly gummed up their wings. With angry gurgles, the gruesome goyles dropped from the sky.

'Yahoo!' cheered Toal. 'Three down, three to go!'

With another flick of a switch, the Buzzard's golden beak creaked open and grabbed one of the other stone imps. It closed around the demon and, like a junkyard car crusher, ground it to gravel!

'*Oooh! Squeak! Honk!*' gurgled the

remaining two in fear, and they bolted away.

'Way to go, Charlie!' cheered Smuts.

'Let's get 'em,' cried Toal, and I steered after the fleeing goyles. We skimmed along just metres from the ground, weaving between outcrops of rock that rose like rotten teeth from the valley floor.

Then I saw a sight that froze the blood in my veins – on top of a massive pillar was a tangled clump of blackened branches. Perched on the nest was the rest of the gruesome goyle gang, perhaps a hundred of the critters, and in the centre sat little Quinn.

'There's my boy!' bellowed Toal. 'Don't worry, Daddy's here!'

The goyles shrieked in alarm. They had been expecting Toal, but not a massive metal bird of prey! I pulled the Buzzard into a steep climb until we reached the top of the cliffs, then turned and dived. We raced down, the wind screaming as it whistled through our metal feathers.

I flicked another switch on the control panel and the Buzzard's legs clanked up underneath; a hatch opened and its feet closed around something inside. The legs

lowered again, revealing a massive saw-
toothed disc clamped between the bird's
metal talons. With a whine, the buzz-saw
started to spin and I steered our flying
destroyer straight at the nest.

Our Deadly Soaring Saw! Bzzzz

A flock of goyles launched themselves for
attack. They were bigger than the last lot
– about my size – and *very* quick. Before I
could dodge them, three landed on one of
our wings and knocked us off-course.

'*Na na, na-na na,*' they chanted, thumbing their long noses at us. The creatures started leaping up and down with devilish delight, making the machine rock dangerously from side to side.

'Clear off, you creeps!' cried Smuts and stepped out onto the wing, brandishing a long, barb-tipped spear.

'Be careful!' I yelled, but although he wobbled like a man on a high wire, the mountain-boy's sense of balance was incredible.

'Come on then, show us what you're made of,' he barked as the goyles crept forward, sticking out their purple tongues and rolling back their lips.

'Pulling faces — is that the best you can do?' taunted Smuts.

Then one of the goyles brayed like a delighted donkey and shot little barbs of deadly lightning from its bulbous eyes. 'Duck!' yelled Toal, and Smuts dropped to his knees, the electric shower fizzing inches over his head. Toal took a mighty

The goyles pulled horrible faces - Oo-er I'm shaking!

swipe with his war hammer and cracked the stone demon's bonce right off! A second goyle came, and then another; Smuts prodded them towards his chief with the spear and, one by one, the mighty warrior whacked their stone heads right across the valley.

'Forty-love,' beamed Toal, swinging his club through the air like a tennis racket. 'Come on, let's be havin' you, you babies!'

But the remaining goyles had taken enough punishment, and raced back to their nest. The Buzzard dived after them as Smuts leaped back into his cockpit. The buzz-saw sang in the air and as we swept over the pillar, it whined and screamed, slicing away a huge chunk of rock that fell amid a shower of rotting branches.

A host of stone demons fell with the cascading rubble. Some ended up stunned on the valley floor; others gave up the fight and raced for freedom. To our amazement we saw a crowd of people emerge from a small cave entrance at the base of the column and chase away the surviving goyles.

'It's the Horroscar men!' cried Toal. 'So *that's* where they've been imprisoned. Get stuck in, lads!' he yelled down.

I turned the machine around and attacked the column again. *Bzzzzz! Zuzzzz!* Another chunk of nest collapsed and another set of shocked goyles scarpered.

'Look at Quinn,' yelled Toal.

The brave baby had lifted a grisly goyle above his head. 'Biffety bop!' we heard the infant cry, but as he launched the struggling statue into the air, two of the remaining goyles grabbed him.

Holding Quinn by his hands and feet, they swung him out over the pillar's edge – once, twice, back and forth over the drop. Oh yikes, the grinning idiots were going to throw him over the side!

I flew our speeding bird straight at them. 'Get ready!' I yelled at Toal and Smuts. 'It's our only chance.' As we raced through the air like fighter pilots, the ghastly goyles threw the child from the pillar.

'Now!' I yelled and flipped the bird-plane

over so we were flying upside down. As we passed above the falling Quinn, first Smuts and then Toal extended their arms, making a desperate grab for the boy. Smuts missed, but Toal managed to grab him in his great arms and hugged him to his chest.

'Fun fun!' crowed the toddler as I righted the Buzzard and sent it screaming up the valley side. The few remaining goyles raced off in the opposite direction, hopefully never to return! As we flew up out of the valley, Toal's clansmen started to climb up the rocks after us.

'We've done it,' beamed Toal, cuddling his son. 'And our men are coming home. Yippee!'

'Well done, Charlie,' cried Smuts, slapping me on the back.

'*Mama!*' gurgled Quinn as we soared to the top of the mountain; below us Megan and the Horroscar women were waving and cheering.

Uh Oh!

Just then I heard a mighty *twang* and our propeller suddenly span to a halt. Oh yikes!

'What's wrong, Charlie?' called Smuts as our bird tilted forward into a nosedive.

'We're going down!' I cried. 'The Buzzard's elastic band has broken.'

I pulled harder, trying to lift our nose, and the huge wings creaked and groaned under the pressure. *Ping!* The Buzzard's wings went floppy. We dropped from the sky like a swatted fly.

Drat! I thought, flicking manically through the Buzzard's manual. What do I do now? IN-FLIGHT CATERING, that's no good I thought and turned the page . . . no . . . aha! What's this? – EJECTOR SEATS!

'Brace yourselves,' I cried and yanked on a handle below my seat.

'What fooooor!' screamed Toal, as our three chairs sprang from the bird with a mighty *ker-ping!*, shooting us into the air.

Up, up, up, we went.

Then down, down, down!

'Charlie!' bellowed Toal Horroscar. 'What have you done?'

'Don't worry!' I cried as we dropped towards the worried crowd below. Then, *Whoosh! Whoosh! Whoosh!* Three parachutes blossomed like huge white flowers from the backs of our seats.

'Phew!' gasped Smuts as we began to drift gently down. 'I thought we were goners!'

'Hurrah!' cheered the waiting crowd below.

'Charlie, you'll get the Horroscar Medal of Honour for this,' beamed Toal.

'Oh, thanks!' I cried, thrilled.

But just then my parachute got caught on a current of warm air, and I was swept up and away from the mountain. 'Come back, Charlie,' called Smuts as they all landed safely on the ground, but there was nothing I could do.

'Cheerio!' I yelled as my chair disappeared into a thick bank of cloud. Up and up and up again, taken by the wind . . .

All of a sudden something jerked my parachute and whisked me out of the cloud. Oh yikes! I found myself staring into the terrifying eyes of a goyle the size of a dragon – and now I am being carried across the sky, dangling from its claws. Where is it taking me? Help, someone, heeeelp!

This is where this scrap of lost journal finishes, but don't worry – a few more pages have just been handed in. To find out if Charlie escapes the giant goyle, go to his website at **www.charliesmall.co.uk**

Look out for Charlie Small's other adventures!

GORILLA CITY

PIRATE GALLEON

THE PUPPET MASTER'S PRISON

DESTINY MOUNTAIN

THE UNDERWORLD

FROSTBITE PASS

THE MUMMY'S TOMB

FOREST OF SKULLS

PLANET OF THE GERKS

Help